LYDIA,

STAY CREATIVE!

Gruel Snarl
Draws a Wild Zugthing

Jeff Jantz

Schiffer Publishing Ltd®

4880 Lower Valley Road • Atglen, PA 19310

To my mom: For encouraging me to do creative things back when I was a wild kid, especially when I was driving her Zonkers!

In an intragalactic dimension,
on the other side of a
ripple in space,

there lived a kid named

Gruel Snarl.

Gruel spent his days doing

"Too Loud!"

all kinds of things:

"I see you!"

playing,

bouncing,

exploring,

and climbing.

"That will break!"

"You know better!"

"I need to find something else for this kid to do!"
thought Gruel's Mom.

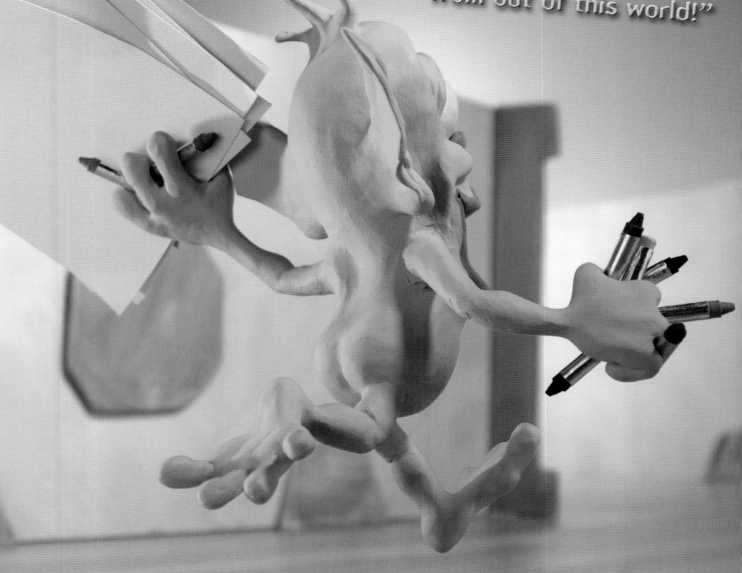

Gruel drew all kinds of **Wild Zugthings**.

A **Zark** and a **Fizz**,
a **Girzaff**,
a **Zake** and **Mouzes**,
an **Elazant**,
and a **Zugrilla**.

"Okay, dear, that sounds **Zoobletastic.**"

Gruel's next drawing was **so** wild that . . .

. . . it *jumped*
right off the **page!!!**

The Wild Zugthing wanted to try

all kinds of things:

playing,

bouncing,

exploring,

and climbing.

"Uhhh, umm. Okay? that sounds **Zoobletastic.**"

While the Zugthing was distracted, Gruel quickly got things back in order.

Meanwhile, back on the other side of a ripple in space,

there **lived** a **kid** . . .

He imagined Gruel—

as Gruel imagined him.

Who's
drawing
who?

Created by

Story by Jeff Jantz
Digital photography supervisor/editor, custom
text, and all around collaborator: Jamie Jantz
Cover design by Brenda McCallum

This book was created with sculptures
made from polymer and modeling clay, wire,
aluminum foil, acrylic paint, wood, paper,
custom 3-D printed objects, and all
kinds of things.

Type set in Ravie/Amoebia/Verdana

ISBN: 978-0-7643-5397-0

Printed in China

Published by Schiffer Publishing, Ltd.
4880 Lower Valley Road
Atglen, PA 19310
Phone: (610) 593-1777; Fax: (610) 593-2002
E-mail: Info@schifferbooks.com
Web: www.schifferbooks.com

For our complete selection of fine books on this
and related subjects, please visit our website at
www.schifferbooks.com. You may also write for
a free catalog.

Schiffer Publishing's titles are available at
special discounts for bulk purchases for sales
promotions or premiums. Special editions,
including personalized covers, corporate
imprints, and excerpts, can be created in
large quantities for special needs. For more
information, contact the publisher.

We are always looking for people to write
books on new and related subjects. If you
have an idea for a book, please contact us at
proposals@schifferbooks.com.